OUTSIDE SHOT

OUTSIDE SHOT

FRED BOWEN

PEACHTREE
ATLANTA

Published by
PEACHTREE PUBLISHERS
1700 Chattahoochee Avenue
Atlanta, Georgia 30318-2112
www.peachtree-online.com

Text © 2017 by Fred Bowen

Edited by Vicky Holifield
Cover design by Nicola Carmack
Composition by Melanie McMahon Ives

Printed in January 2017 in the United States of America by LCS
Communications in Harrisonburg, Virginia
10 9 8 7 6 5 4 3 2 1
First Edition

978-1-56145-955-1 (hardcover)
978-1-56145-956-8 (trade paperback)

Library of Congress Cataloging-in-Publication Data

Names: Bowen, Fred, author.
Title: Outside shot / Fred Bowen.
Description: First edition. | Atlanta, Georgia : Peachtree Publishers, [2017]
  | Series: Fred Bowen sports story | Summary: "Richie Mallon has always
  known he was a shooter. Now that he is facing basketball tryouts under a
  tough new coach, will his amazing shooting talent be enough to keep him on
  the team?"— Provided by publisher.
Identifiers: LCCN 2016025755| ISBN 9781561459551 | ISBN 9781561459568
Subjects: | CYAC: Basketball—Fiction. | Ability—Fiction.
Classification: LCC PZ7.B6724 Ov 2017 | DDC [Fic]—dc23 LC record avail-
able at *https://lccn.loc.gov/2016025755*

For Alice Margaret Bowen,
Little Sis

CHAPTER 1

I'm the shooter.

That's what I do. That's who I am.

When the basketball leaves my hands, it's going in the bucket. I just know it. Not *every* time—not even Stephen Curry is that good—but most of the time.

Don't ask me where I got my ability to shoot hoops. I sure didn't inherit it. My mom and dad are great, but they couldn't care less about sports. Dad's a college English professor. He spends his time reading Shakespeare instead of the sports section. Mom's a pediatrician. She says she has more important stuff to think about than putting a ball in a hoop.

My older sister Jeanie might have been a good player if she'd ever tried, but she's into high school musicals and stuff like that. She doesn't have time for sports. I don't think she could throw a ball into the ocean if she was standing knee-deep in the water.

No, I got to be great at shooting another way. Practice. A whole lot of practice.

When I was eight years old we moved into the house where we live now. There was a regulation ten-foot basketball hoop in the driveway. I was new to the neighborhood and I didn't know anybody. That basketball hoop was my best friend.

Even though I've always been pretty big for my age, I had trouble getting the ball in the basket at first. But I kept at it. I practiced all the time, trying to learn the shots I'd seen on TV. I spent hours and hours shooting hoops. Playing games in my head.

Finally I worked out a shot of my own. I would dribble up the right side of the driveway to get a running start and sling the ball up from my right hip. Man, I never missed that one.

After a few months our next-door neighbor, Mrs. Moore, looked over the fence. "I declare, Richie Mallon," she called out. "You are getting awfully good at shooting that basketball."

After that, I practiced even harder.

I kept at it and a couple of years later Bryce Cooper—he's my best friend now—asked me to sign up with his basketball team at the recreation center. Mr. Petty was our coach and a really nice guy. He was a huge North Carolina Tar Heels fan.

Anyway, at the start of our first game I got the ball and dribbled down the right side just like I was back in my driveway. I pushed the ball up from my right hip and—

Swish!

The next time I got the ball I did the exact same thing. Nothing but net.

As we were running back to play defense, the other team's coach leaped up, pointed at me, and yelled, "Who's got the shooter?"

The shooter.

I liked the sound of that.

He was talking about me.

CHAPTER 2

I feel great. I could run all day. It's a cool, bright November Sunday. Most people would call this "football weather," but Bryce and I are running to get in shape for our middle school basketball team.

We're running side-by-side along a dirt path that winds for three miles through the trees in Stone Creek Park. The leaves are gone, so we can see the creek for most of the run.

"Hey, watch out for the rocks," Bryce warns. "You don't want to turn an ankle the day before basketball tryouts."

"You got that right. No way I'm going to get hurt and miss tryouts!"

We run along a bridge that crosses the

creek and veer to the right. The path is steeper as it climbs deeper into the woods. Bryce matches every one of my strides.

"Have you heard anything about this new coach, Mr. Sheridan?" I ask.

Bryce shakes his head. "Not much. Davonn says he played ball in college somewhere."

"He must know his stuff." I sidestep a rock and get down to what I'm really thinking about. "I wonder how tough he is."

Bryce doesn't seem too worried. "We'll find out."

I lean into the hill as I run. This is the part of the path that zigzags through the woods and away from the creek. The toughest part of the trail.

I'm still thinking about basketball tryouts. "I wonder how many guys he'll keep."

Again, Bryce is cool. "What do you care?" he says. "You'll make it. You're the best shooter we've got."

I know I'm the best shooter on the team, but still it's nice to hear Bryce say it. I push higher and harder into the hill. "I was just wondering."

"I figure he'll keep about twelve guys," Bryce says. "You need at least ten so you can scrimmage in practice and a couple more in case somebody gets hurt."

Then he starts naming names. I quietly compare them to the list I've been carrying around in my head for weeks.

"He'll keep Davonn, me, you, Mason, Grady Lin, Tony Delgado—"

"Think he'll pick Rick Sullivan?"

"Sully? I don't know. He's not that good."

"Coach has got to keep some seventh graders or he won't have a team next year."

Bryce agrees. "Ray Burns can handle the ball. Charles Jackson and Theo Kirshner can play."

"C. J. isn't that good of a shooter." I haven't told Bryce, but I'm worried about Charles Jackson. He's about my size and plays shooting guard. He might take some of my playing time.

"Yeah, but C. J. is good at everything else and his shot's coming around," Bryce responds. "Coaches like guys who pass and play defense."

I don't even want to think about that. If C. J. starts shooting better, he'll take my spot. *I'm* supposed to be the shooter on this team.

We reach the top of the path where a brown wooden sign sits at the end of the trail. The sign says "Western Ridge" and points in two directions. Without missing a beat Bryce and I head toward the right, the same path we've been running for weeks.

The land rolls gently along. This is an easier part of the trail. I pick up the pace. I'm testing myself for the times late in the fourth quarter when you're so tired you think your legs are going to drop off and you can't run anymore. Bryce falls into step with me.

"We should be pretty good this year," he says, letting me know he's not running so hard he can't talk.

"Pretty good? Are you kidding me?" I shoot him a look. "We're going to be awesome. We've got Davonn. He's going to be the best player in the conference. You and Mason are going to dominate the boards. Grady can handle the ball. And *I* am going to shoot the lights out!"

We slip around two women walking their dogs. "We're going to have a much better record than last year," I declare. "We're gonna blow by 6–4. We may go 10–0."

"Okay, okay," says Bryce. "Chill out. We'll be better."

We fall into an easy stretch as the trail slopes down a hill. Bryce sounded a little annoyed. I shrug it off. Even if Bryce has his doubts, I'm sure we're going to have a big year. Especially me. I'm ready to go.

When we started running a few weeks ago, I would have been completely gassed at this point of the trail. I remember huffing and puffing during our first run. Bryce was even worse.

But now...nothing. I'm not even winded. It's like I can't get tired. I can run—and shoot—forever.

Still, I can't stop thinking about Coach Sheridan.

"So you didn't hear anything about how

tough this guy Sheridan was supposed to be?" I ask as we scramble up another hill.

"Davonn said he talked to one kid who had him in class over at Kennedy High School."

"What does he teach?"

"Math, I think."

"What did the kid say?"

"He said Sheridan was a really tough grader."

I step past another rock on the trail. "Just because a guy is a tough grader in class doesn't mean he's going to be a tough coach."

Bryce shoots me one of those do-you-really-believe-that looks. "I guess we'll find out tomorrow," he says.

I sprint down the trail, surprising Bryce and leaving him in my dust.

I'm ready.

CHAPTER 3

Looks like I'm not in as good shape as I thought.

I stand at the water fountain just outside the gym during a break at the tryouts taking deep breaths, trying to get my wind back. I lean over and take another huge gulp of cold water.

"Hurry up, Mallon!" Davonn shouts from the line. "The rest of us want some water too, you know."

I step aside and Jake Keane, another eighth grader, takes a couple of slow sips, then straightens up. "I quit," he announces. "I can't even take one day of this. No way I can take four months of it."

Jake isn't kidding. He steps into the gym and waves at Coach Sheridan. "I'm quitting, Coach," he says with a big smile. "See you around campus!" He walks back out and bounces down the steps to the locker room. He looks as happy as a kid on Christmas morning.

Coach Sheridan doesn't move a muscle. Just stands there with his arms crossed. It's like Jake had never stepped foot into the gym. He's gone and forgotten.

Bryce stands next to me while we wait for the rest of the Plaza Middle School basketball hopefuls to get back from the water break.

"Well, we know one thing," Bryce whispers to me.

"What's that?"

"Coach Sheridan's plenty tough."

Bryce is right. So far, the first day of tryouts has been murder. Wind sprints. Layup drills. Defensive drills where you scramble back and forth, legs pumping every which way while in your defensive stance—I thought my thighs were going to explode on that one. Coach Sheridan never gives us a minute to catch our breath. He runs us the whole time. No letup.

But it's nothing I can't handle. I should make the team, no problem.

A couple of the seventh graders are better than I thought. Ray Burns is small, but he can really handle the ball. Link Jones seems to grow an inch every time you blink your eyes. He's got to be six-foot-two, and he's getting better every time he touches the ball.

And although I hate to admit it, Charles Jackson's shot has improved. It's not as good as mine, but it's getting better.

Coach blows his whistle and everyone gathers around. He's about six feet tall and built like a brick wall. He's got short black hair. It's not in a military cut, but it's seriously short, especially along the sides—a real no-nonsense look. Standing there in his gray shorts and blue Plaza Middle School T-shirt, Coach looks like he wouldn't have any trouble going full court with us.

"All right, let's finish up with a two-minute shooting drill. We're going to do this at the end of every practice." He starts pacing the gym floor. "I want three guys at each of the baskets. Two guys rebounding for one shooter. The shooter has to move to a new spot after every shot."

Coach motions for Davonn to pass him the ball. He flips up a quick jump shot.

Swish.

"Now move to a new spot, like this." Coach shuffles over several steps. Davonn tosses him a pass. Coach flips up another jumper with a smooth flick of the wrist.

Swish.

"Keep moving. Catch it. Shoot it. Go to another spot. Catch it. Shoot it. Spot up. Remember, square your shoulders to the basket on each shot. Follow through with your wrist."

Coach Sheridan takes three more shots. Nothing but net every time. The guy never misses.

"Okay, groups of three at all the baskets," Coach Sheridan says. "Move it."

Bryce and I jog over to a side basket with Anthony Delgado. "Maybe you aren't the best shooter on the team after all," Bryce whispers as he glances back at Coach Sheridan. "That guy's good."

"No doubt about it," I say under my breath. "Of course, maybe a shooter like him will appreciate someone who can shoot."

"Keep track of how many shots you make in the two minutes," Coach says, "and report the scores to Camila and Madison."

Camila Garcia and Madison Gray are our team managers. They're going to keep all the stats for Coach Sheridan. And so far it looks like he keeps track of everything. How many layups you make. How many you miss. Every good pass and every time you mess up. I just hope they put down some good numbers for me.

Bryce goes first from our group. He's not a great shooter. He's more of a rebounder who gets most of his buckets close to the hoop. Bryce scores twelve baskets in his two minutes. Not bad, not great.

Anthony is next. He gets ten.

It's my turn. Now's my chance to show Sheridan what I can do. If I'm going to be a starter, I've got to show him I can shoot the ball.

Coach looks at his watch. "Everybody ready?" he asks. He counts down. "Three... two..."

I take a couple of deep breaths.

"Go!"

My first shot feels good, but bounces off the back of the iron. Too long. I'm too pumped up. The second shot is short. The third is another miss. I feel my heart jumping around in my chest.

Nice and smooth, I remind myself. The next shot rattles around the rim and drops in. I'm on the board.

"One!" Bryce shouts.

I know the next shot is in as soon as it leaves my hand. "Two."

Now I'm in my rhythm. The baskets begin to fall one after another.

Swish.

Swish.

Around the rim and in.

The count goes higher and higher. "Seven... eight...nine..."

I'm smoking hot now. I can't miss.

"Twelve...thirteen...fourteen..."

When a shot bounces off, I'm shocked. Bryce grabs the rebound and gets me back on track right away.

Swish.

"Fifteen."

"Thirty seconds to go!" Coach Sheridan shouts.

My next shot bangs off the rim and bounds toward the corner. I follow the ball, holding out my hands. "Left wing!" I yell, and Bryce hooks a no-look pass over his head right to me.

In the air...in the bucket.

"Sixteen."

By now my legs are burning. Man, I wish I had started running with Bryce earlier in the fall.

Swish.

"Seventeen."

I can feel the time dripping away.

Swish.

"Eighteen."

Coach starts counting down the time, like

the home crowd at a big game. "Ten...nine...eight..."

I'm not sure of my next shot. My legs are so tired I feel like I'm pushing the ball instead of shooting it.

Around the rim and in.

"Nineteen."

"Get me the ball, get me the ball!" I shout, moving to a final spot.

"Four...three...two..."

Bryce flicks me a two-handed chest pass. The ball barely touches my hands before it's in the air. Coach blows his whistle as the ball starts down toward the basket. The ball splashes though the net.

"Yes!" I punch the air with my fist.

"Count it, Mallon," Coach says. I notice the smallest smile at the corner of his mouth. I'm pretty sure he knows I'm the shooter.

Camila walks over with her clipboard. "How many?" she asks.

"Twenty."

"Twenty?" she repeats, looking at Bryce.

Bryce nods. "Twenty, Cammy. Write it down. My man's the shooter."

"Pretty good," she says as she marks it on her chart.

"How many did Davonn have?" I ask.

"Eighteen." Cammy flashes me a grin as she shows me the chart. She just got her braces off and I can tell she knows she has a killer smile.

TWO-MINUTE DRILL

Player	Shots Made
Davonn Peters	18
Rick Sullivan	8
Peter Washington	7
Scott Hamilton	11
Bryce Cooper	12
Anthony DelGado	10
Richie Mallon	20

"Don't worry, you're the best," she says.

I already know that. I just hope Coach knows it.

CHAPTER 4

I hear the school bell ring as I hop off the bus. We only have three days left until Thanksgiving break. I can't wait.

I hurry through the double doors and spot Bryce leaning against the wall with his head in his phone. The only things moving are his thumbs. And they're moving a mile a minute.

"What's up? Aren't you going to history class?"

"Madison just texted me," Bryce says, keeping his eyes glued to his phone. "Sheridan posted—"

Bryce doesn't have to say another word. I know what he's talking about. Coach Sheridan has posted the list of players who have made the team. Suddenly my mouth is dry and my heart is pounding. I'm 99 percent sure I'm going to make the team. It's the other 1 percent that's killing me.

I whip out my phone and start working the keys. My mind is working even faster than my thumbs. *Sheridan's got to take me. I'm the shooter. I got the highest scores in most of the two-minute drills. Once I got twenty-three baskets. I think that's a record for the team. And I've been pretty good in the scrimmages. I'm not Davonn. But who is?*

"I made it!" Bryce yells, thrusting both hands into the air.

"Wait. I haven't got to the website yet," I say, still punching the keys. My thumb hits the wrong button and the screen goes blank.

"Arrrgh! Give me your phone!" I grab Bryce's phone and scroll down the list and look at my life for the next four months. I skip by the first couple of names. They hardly register in my brain. Finally, near the bottom of the list, I see what I'm searching for: my name, Richie Mallon.

I let out a deep breath. Now I can study the rest of the list.

RAY BURNS
BRYCE COOPER
ANTHONY DELGADO
MASON GREGG
SCOTT HAMILTON
CHARLES JACKSON
LINCOLN JONES
THEO KIRSHNER
GRADY LIN
RICHIE MALLON
QUINTON MCDANIEL
DAVONN PETERS

I give Bryce a shoulder bump. Yes! We've made the team.

"I told you not to worry." Bryce points at the list. "Hey, look," he whispers. "Sully didn't make it." He makes it sound as if not making the team is like having a disease or something.

"Yeah, I thought he might make it instead of Scott."

It's tough. Thirty kids tried out and only twelve made it. The truth is that a whole bunch of kids are disappointed while eleven other kids and I are really happy.

Bryce and I head off to history class. I can't stop smiling all morning.

A funny thing happens at lunchtime. For the last couple of weeks, all the guys trying out for the basketball team have been sitting at the same lunch table every day, talking hoops, having fun. Well, today the guys who didn't make the list go to another table. Nobody says anything—it's not like the guys who made the team kick them out or anything. It just happens.

Near the end of practice another weird thing happens. Coach brings everybody together, and I figure he's going to yell at us or make us run defensive drills again.

Instead, he asks everyone to sit in a circle and tell the team something about themselves. "If you guys are going to be teammates," he says, "you should know something about each other besides basketball statistics. A team should be like a family."

Most of the kids talk about regular stuff like where they live or who their favorite basketball team or player is. But some other players say things that stick with me.

Davonn says his dad was born in Senegal, a country in West Africa. His parents met when his dad came over to America to study.

Both of Grady's parents were born in Japan but moved to America when they were teenagers. They still speak Japanese at home.

"That's great," Coach Sheridan says. "I wish I knew a second language."

Anthony says that he and his little brother live in the Ashworth Apartments over near the railroad tracks with his grandparents. Anthony's dad left years ago and his mother has problems, but he doesn't say what.

Link's mom has some kind of nerve disease that flares up sometimes. "She may come to the games with a cane or a walker," he says, "and she'll probably sit in the first row because it's hard for her to climb the steps." Then he laughs and adds, "But her voice is fine. You'll hear her all over the gym. She's a screamer."

Coach smiles. "Ask her to please come to as many games as she feels up to. We need all the fans we can get."

Bryce tells us about how his youngest brother has autism. "It's not really bad," he says, like he's trying to protect him. "But he can act a little funny sometimes and he's got to go to a special school."

When it's my turn, I'm not sure what to say. I have it pretty easy compared to Tony and Link and some of the other guys. So I tell everybody about how I moved into town when I was eight. I also tell them about all the time I spent shooting at the basketball hoop in the driveway—my best friend.

"I guess that's why you're a good shooter," Coach Sheridan says.

I like hearing that.

Finally, after all the players have said something, Grady looks at Coach Sheridan and asks, "What about you, Coach? We need to know something about you."

"Well, let's see. I played college hoops at St. Thomas University, a Division III school in Minnesota," he says. Then he gets a funny grin on his face. "But the big news is my wife is expecting twins."

"When?" Davonn asks.

"In late March," Coach says, "hopefully after the season is over."

CHAPTER 5

Coach Sheridan keeps talking about how a basketball team is like a family. But man, if this is how he treats his family, I feel sorry for those twins.

For the past couple of weeks, practices have been brutal. Today he starts us with layup drills. But not just straight boring layups like you did when you were ten years old. No way. I'm talking Sheridan layups. Balls buzzing back and forth all over the gym. Everybody running full speed. No slowing down. No resting.

He has us do every kind of layup you can imagine. Right hand, left hand, right side, left side, and coming underneath the bucket and spinning the ball off the backboard.

"Got to practice them with both hands and different ways!" Coach shouts. "The other team isn't going to let you walk in and score an easy layup."

Then it's fast break drills. I weave down the court at top speed with two other guys, moving and passing. Then I catch the ball on the fly and lay it in the basket. I'm gassed, but I turn around and do it again.

Next we do what Coach calls "in and out drills." A player passes the ball to a teammate near the basket, then that guy whips it back so the first player can take an outside shot. Pass it inside, whip it back outside. In and out. In and out.

Coach is constantly in our ears about proper shooting form. "Get the ball up quick. Square your shoulders to the basket…every time. Good release. Follow through with your wrist."

But Coach isn't finished with us yet. I feel sick when he motions for Madison to bring out the dreaded orange plastic cones for one of his "quickness drills."

They're the worst, the absolute worst. Coach sets out six pairs of orange plastic cones. You have to sprint to the first cone and then crouch down in a defensive position and shuffle your feet sideways as fast as you can to the second cone. It's about twenty feet away, but it seems like a hundred. Then you have to sprint to the second set of cones and the third and do the same thing. After that you cross over to the other side of the court and repeat the drill with another three sets of cones.

This drill is a killer. I can make it through without stumbling or passing out, but believe me, when I'm done my legs are burning and my tongue is hanging out.

I hate those orange cones!

While we're being tormented on the court, Cammy and Madison keep track of everything. Every basket, every miss, and every time you mess up. They mark it all down in notebooks to show Sheridan after we head down to the showers. Sheridan is big into notebooks.

When practice is over I hang back and

walk slowly past the managers' table, hoping to get a peek at the stats. Madison shuts her notebook, hands it to Cammy, and heads toward the door. "See you later," she says to Cammy.

I edge closer to get a look at Cammy's book, but she pulls it toward her.

"Can I get a quick look at my stats?" I ask.

She covers them up like she's guarding the answers to a math quiz. "Looking at them won't change anything," she says. "Just keep playing the game." She slams her book shut and hurries off after Madison.

This is not good. Why wouldn't she want me to see my stats? She's shown them to me before. Is she mad at me or something? Or maybe she doesn't want me to see them because after two weeks of practices my stats aren't that good?

Coach has had me playing with the second string most of the time. He tries to put a positive spin on it. "I'm just trying out different combinations," he tells me. "I want more scoring coming off the bench."

Bryce tells me the same things, thinking

he's encouraging me. But I'm not so sure. The bench is the bench.

I'd much rather be playing with the first team. Davonn is so good that the defense is all over him, but he can dish the ball off to me for a million wide-open jumpers. That's great for a shooter.

But instead I'm stuck on the second team playing against the first string in scrimmages. And things are even worse when we're on defense. Sometimes I have to cover—or should I say *try* to cover—Davonn. No way I can stick with that guy. He's so strong, skinny, and quick that he's like a snake or something. He always finds a way to slither his way to the basket.

Charles Jackson usually covers me in scrimmages. He's not as good a shooter as I am, but like Bryce said, he's good at everything else, especially defense. Maybe that's why Coach has him on the first team instead of me.

Today's the last day of practice before the season's first game. When we come out of the locker room, Cammy and Madison are handing out the game schedules.

PLAZA MIDDLE SCHOOL KNIGHTS—
BOYS BASKETBALL

Date	Opponent	Time
December 7	Burr MS	4 p.m.
December 14	@ Saratoga MS	4 p.m.
January 4	Fair Hill MS	4 p.m.
January 11	@ Culbert MS	4 p.m.
January 18	Stone Mill MS	4 p.m.
January 25	@ Burr MS	4 p.m.
February 1	Saratoga MS	4 p.m.
February 8	@ Fair Hill MS	4 p.m.
February 15	Culbert MS	4 p.m.
February 22	@ Stone Mill MS	4 p.m.

I stand there for a minute, staring at the schedule.

"What are you looking at?" Bryce asks. "It's only ten games. It's not like it's going to change or something."

"I don't know. I just think schedules are cool."

"Why?"

"They're like...looking at a map before you go on a trip."

"What are you talking about?" he asks.

"You know, you see the names of the places, but you don't know what they'll be like."

Bryce looks at me like I'm a little crazy. "Well, I know we're going to beat Stone Mill," he says. "They're never very good."

"Yeah, maybe. But you don't *really* know that." I look the schedule up and down one last time.

"First game tomorrow," Bryce says as he turns to head toward the locker room.

I smile. "Let the trip begin."

CHAPTER 6

I can't say I'm crazy about sitting on the bench. I know it's supposed to be all about the team, but when Coach Sheridan announced the starting lineup before the game I had a hard time feeling all rah-rah about it.

"Peters," Coach called out, "Gregg, Lin, Cooper, and...Jackson."

I have to admit it really hurt hearing C. J.'s name. I almost couldn't look at Bryce. I mean, we've been talking about starting together since we began running in Stone Creek Park.

But I suck it up and make sure I sit right next to Coach on the bench. I don't want him to forget me.

It seems like forever, but it's only four minutes into the game when I get the call.

"Mallon, go in for C. J."

Coach doesn't have to tell me twice. I almost run to the scorer's table.

"Looks like Coach is bringing in the shooter," Cammy says as I kneel in front of the table. I can't tell if she's teasing me or what, but it doesn't matter right now. I take a couple of deep breaths, glance at the scoreboard, and pray for a stoppage of play.

Tweeeeeeeeet! The whistle blows. I'm in.

Coming into a game off the bench is tough. Much tougher than starting. It's like jumping into a rushing river or something. Everyone else is warmed up and the game is moving fast and you've got to catch up, quick.

I get my first chance early. Davonn drives hard to the basket. The Burr defense double-teams him, cutting off his path to the bucket. Davonn flips a pass to me on the left wing, my favorite spot. I've taken this shot a million times in my driveway, at the park, and in practice.

I don't hesitate. A shooter's got to shoot.
Swish!

I point to Davonn and mouth the words "nice pass" as we run back on defense. Bryce makes a fist. I see Cammy marking down the basket in the scorebook.

Now I feel like I'm really in the game.

We grab a lead in the first half, but Burr makes a run at us in the second half to pull within two points. Davonn hits a twisting layup and sets me up for a couple of wide-open jump shots to help us pull away.

The Burr coach calls for a timeout. I look up at the scoreboard as we walk off the court.

We're leading by six points with three minutes to go.

"C. J., report in for Mallon."

I figure Coach is putting C. J. in for his defense.

Then he gives the rest of us another one of his little pep talks. "Stay with what we've been doing. Move it around. Take good shots. Remember, we've got the lead. If we rebound and play good defense, we'll win this game."

Coach taps the seat next to him as I go back to the bench. "Stay close by," he tells me. "I may put you back in if we need a basket." I sit *really* close to him. I'm not in his lap or anything, but if there wasn't so much noise in the gym I could hear him breathing.

Sure enough, after a Burr basket that cuts the lead to four, Coach puts me in for C. J. "Look for your shot!" he shouts as I trot onto the court.

Grady's watching for Davonn, but the Burr defense has Davonn smothered. So he passes the ball to me on the left wing. I glance underneath the basket for Mason. He's covered too. Bryce sets a pick near the foul line on my right. I fake left and cut hard to the right, running the defender into Bryce.

I'm open for a second, but that's all I need. I power up for the jump shot. The ball bounces around the rim and falls in. We're up by six again. Coach can breathe easier now.

We trade buckets and hang on to win our first game of the season.

Coach isn't as happy as I expected him to be. He hardly cracks a smile as he talks to us. "Not bad for the first game. We did some good things. I like the defense. I like the hustle. But we've got a lot of stuff to work on. Be ready to come to practice next week and work hard."

I can't tell you how many times I've heard coaches say that. My guess is we'll be seeing a lot of the dreaded orange cones next week.

After trading fist bumps with Bryce, I wander over to the scorer's table "Can I see the stats?" I ask Cammy.

She gives me that same disappointed look as the other day. "Check the scoreboard," she says, all serious like. "We won. That's the only stat that matters, right?"

Cammy's getting to be a pain. I look up. The lights on the scoreboard are off. The players are on their way to the locker room and the fans are heading home.

"I forgot the final score."

She shakes her head as if she knows I'm lying and spins the scorebook toward me.

Player	FGs	FTs	Rebs	Assists	Points
Davonn Peters	5/12	4/6	8	2	14
Bryce Cooper	2/6	1/2	5	1	5
Mason Gregg	2/2	0/2	4	0	4
Charles Jackson	1/5	2/2	1	2	4
Grady Lin	2/5	0/0	0	3	5
Richie Mallon	4/5	1/2	0	0	9
Theo Kirshner	1/1	0/0	2	0	2
Anthony Delgado	0/0	0/0	2	0	0
Quinton McDaniel	0/0	0/0	1	1	0
Ray Burns	1/1	0/0	0	2	3
Totals:	**18/36**	**8/14**	**23**	**11**	**46**

3-point goals: Lin (1); Burns (1)

I check out my line. Nine points.

Only Davonn scored more than me. I only missed one shot—that's 80 percent shooting. If I'd made that second free throw I could have scored double figures. Not too bad.

"You're taking a long time to figure out we won 46–40," Cammy says.

"So I'm not that great at math."

"Then what are you doing in the top math class with me?"

I don't have an answer for that one. "Thanks," I say and take a step toward the door that leads to the locker room.

"You know, there's more to the game than just shooting and scoring points." Then she gives me a weird little smile.

"Then why does the team with the most points always win?" I ask.

I turn and take off for the locker room, replaying each of my baskets in my memory.

CHAPTER 7

My mom may not care much for basketball, but she sure is crazy about Christmas. I think it's because she works so much. She feels like she's got to do Christmas up big. Dad's the same way.

So our family has a million holiday traditions. The biggest one is buying the tree. We're not one of those families that goes to a Christmas tree place set up in a parking lot and says, "Hey, the one on the end looks good, tie it to the car."

No way. In our family, a couple of weeks before Christmas everybody gets together to choose the perfect tree. My parents take a day off and Mom writes notes for Jeanie and me to be excused from school for "a family event." That's how serious she is about it.

We drive way out into the country to a Christmas tree farm where we can cut down our own tree. I mean *way* out. I'm not even sure some of these places get cell phone reception.

This year we're trying out a new tree farm. We drive for, like, two hours, into the middle of nowhere. We play Christmas songs from mom's playlist the whole way. Mom and Jeanie sing along. I mostly stare out the window and think about basketball.

As we're winding our way through the woods I ask, "Why don't we cut one of *these* trees down? There sure are a lot of them." Nobody responds. I guess you can't just pull off the road and cut down any old tree for Christmas. So I go back to staring at the countryside.

Finally we turn onto a dirt road with so many potholes I'm positive the car is going to disappear into one. A sign reads "Anderson Tree Farm."

We get out of the car. It's colder out here than it is where we live. There are trees growing in neat rows as far as I can see.

A woman comes out of the farmhouse. She's tall, even taller than me, and dressed in a red plaid shirt and jeans. She looks to be about as old as my grandparents. Two golden retrievers bound out of the house with her. They race by us and into the field.

"What can I do for you?" she asks in a friendly voice.

"We're here to buy a tree," my father says.

The woman laughs. "I think we can help you there. We have acres of them."

"Where are your Douglas firs?" Mom asks.

The woman turns and points. "Over there. The last five rows. Do you need a saw or a canvas for pulling back the tree?"

"No thanks," Dad says, shaking his head. "We've got it covered. We've done this before."

"Well then, you know what to do. Find one you like. Cut it down as close to the ground as you can. Drag it back to the barn and we'll settle up. By the way, I'm Dorothy Anderson. Folks call me Dot."

"Thanks, Dot."

Ms. Anderson looks at the clouds moving swiftly across the sky. "Wind is up this afternoon. It's getting cold. I'll make some cocoa for all of us."

As we walk among the trees, the dogs scramble after us. "How big do we want the tree to be?" Jeanie asks.

"About seven feet," Mom answers.

I hold my hand above my head. "So, about this tall?"

"How tall are you?" Jeanie asks.

"Five-eleven."

"You're not five-eleven."

"I am," I insist. "I got measured at basketball tryouts."

"In your shoes?" Jeanie asks.

"Of course. Nobody plays hoop in their bare feet."

"You're five-ten at the most," Jeanie says and walks away. Just like a big sister.

We look at a bunch of trees. Mom vetoes all of them. They're either too skinny or too wide or they have something else wrong with them.

I wander off with the dogs. They're just the kind of big, friendly, slobbery dogs I wish I could have. But Dad's allergic to dogs. Or so he says.

I turn a corner and see the perfect tree. Not too skinny, not too wide. I walk over and reach up. My hand just touches the top.

"Hey, over here!" I shout. "I found it."

Mom takes one look and agrees. "It's perfect." She gives me a big hug, then looks straight at me and whispers, "I bet you must be at least five-eleven." I like the sound of that.

Dad saws through the trunk near the bottom, wraps the tree in the canvas sheet we brought along, and heads back toward the barn, dragging the tree behind him. The air is crisp and the smell of the evergreens surrounds us. I'm glad we drove for hours instead of going to a parking lot to get our tree.

Ms. Anderson is waiting at the barn. "So you found one you like?" she calls out.

"A perfect seven-foot Douglas fir," Dad says. "What do we owe you?"

"Does fifty dollars sound fair to you?"

Dad nods and hands over the money.

"Have some cocoa before we tie the tree to your car," Ms. Anderson insists.

She fills four red mugs and hands one to each of us. The steam rises. It feels good to hold the warm mug in my cold hands.

Jeanie takes a sip. "This is wonderful."

"Thanks. It's the real thing. I make it from scratch with real cocoa. I never did like that instant stuff."

Mom and Dad talk with Ms. Anderson about a bunch of things. Tree farming. Living in the country. Her dogs. I'm barely listening as I look around the barn.

Then I see it. Ten feet above the dirt floor of the barn, a basketball hoop darkened with age is sticking right out from the barn wall.

"Who plays hoop?" I ask, pointing at the old rim.

Ms. Anderson looks up and smiles. "I did. In high school...a long, long time ago."

"Were you any good?"

"Richie!" Mom says. She thinks I'm being a wise guy or something.

"I just asked because she's tall and looks like she'd be good."

"Oh, that's okay," Ms. Anderson says. "I loved the game. I was a good shooter. I once scored sixty-two points in a game."

"Sixty-two points?" The number stuns me. "In one game?"

"Well, you've got to remember that those were the old days when girls played six-on-six basketball. They split the court in two parts. Some of the girls just played offense and some girls just played defense. I played offense because I was tall, so all I did was shoot. I didn't even have to play defense."

"I'm the shooter on my team too," I say.

Ms. Anderson stares off at the old rim. "I never learned to do much else. It was hard to dribble on this stuff," she says, scuffing her boot against the dirt floor of the barn. "And living so far out in the country I was all by myself so I had nobody to pass to."

She pours herself a cup of cocoa and takes a sip. She looks around the barn, and her eyes stop again on the old rim.

"It's best to learn all the parts of the

game," she says, speaking directly to me. "Don't be just a shooter."

I smile and lick some cocoa from my top lip. "I'll try to remember that, the next game we play."

But I don't really mean it. I like being the shooter.

CHAPTER 8

We find out one thing quickly: Saratoga Middle School's team is a lot better than Burr's.

They're a step quicker, so they seem to be everywhere at once. Every basket is a struggle for us. They play a collapsing zone that blankets Davonn anytime he gets the ball.

Coach Sheridan grabs me early in the game. "Go in for C. J.," he says. "Find a soft spot in their zone and take some shots."

I bounce up from the bench and pull my warm-up jersey off over my head. This is one of my jobs on the team: zone breaker. The shooter is always a zone breaker. A good zone won't let anyone take shots close to the basket. But a good shooter can get outside shots against a zone. And that's where I come in.

I don't get off to a great start. Grady passes the ball to me on the wing. I'm open, so I shoot. The ball feels good leaving my hand but bounces off the rim.

I miss my second shot too.

It's funny how a couple of missed shots can play with your head. The next time I get the ball, I pass it back to Grady.

Saratoga grabs an early lead and holds on through the first half. With only fifteen seconds left, Davonn drives to the basket. The Saratoga zone cuts off his path to the bucket, so Davonn dishes the ball to me on the left wing.

I'm open. I force myself to concentrate. *Don't think about the misses.* This time I stay squared to the basket and smooth all the way through the shot.

Swish!

Saratoga tries to score one more time before the half, but the three-pointer circles the rim and doesn't go in. I glance at the scoreboard as both teams leave the gym. At least I got one basket.

Coach is pretty calm, considering we're behind by four. He paces back and forth as we take our water break, but when we gather around, he doesn't yell at us.

"We're playing well," he says. "Keep it up. We're working hard on defense. Mason and Bryce are doing a good job on the boards. Keep the ball moving around their zone. You beat a zone by passing, not dribbling. That means you, Davonn. Don't be afraid to take an outside shot if you're open. Just like in the shooting drill."

As the second half begins, I'm half hoping Coach might start me so I can be the zone breaker.

Instead…surprise. I'm on the bench again. Bummer.

Even worse, C. J. hits a couple of jumpers to pull us even. The hoops help the team, but they're keeping me on the bench. If C. J. hits his shots, Coach doesn't have any reason to put me in the game.

Finally he puts me in. But the long break has cooled me off. I miss some more shots. Before long I'm parked on the bench again.

We trade the lead back and forth. Neither team can pull very far ahead. With about two minutes to go, a Saratoga guard lets a long shot fly from behind the three-point line. It smacks off the backboard and falls right in the basket. Three points!

I fall back on the bench. What a lucky shot. We're behind, 42–39.

But we bounce right back. Davonn squeezes through two Saratoga defenders and banks a twisting layup off the glass. Two points! We're behind 42–41 with fifty seconds to go.

Everyone on the bench is leaning forward. Coach Sheridan's on his feet, shouting instructions. "Play good D! Move your feet!"

I look at the clock...40 seconds...39...38...

Saratoga moves the ball around. They'll be happy to run out the clock and hold on to their one-point lead.

C. J. almost gets his hands on a cross-court pass, but Saratoga holds on.

The clock ticks down...23...22...21...

Coach Sheridan jumps up and starts waving his hands. "Foul them!" he shouts. "Foul them!"

C. J. darts out and slaps at the ball. He smacks a Saratoga guard's arm instead.

Tweeeeeeeet! The whistle stops the play. "Foul on number 24," the referee calls. The horn blows at the scorer's table. "One and one," the scorer signals. The Saratoga guard steps to the foul line.

I do a quick calculation in my head. *If he makes at least one foul shot, we'll need a bucket to tie and a three-pointer to win. But if he misses, we'll only need a two-pointer to win.*

The referee hands the ball to the Saratoga player. "The ball is in play," he instructs the players along the lane.

The Saratoga player takes a deep breath and dribbles the ball three times.

Thump...thump...thump.

He shoots. From the bench the shot looks good. But the ball grazes the front rim, plunks off the back, and rattles out.

Bryce grabs the rebound and looks around. Coach is off the bench in a flash. "Timeout!" he shouts, forming a T with his hands.

He grabs me and says, "Report in for C. J." I run to the scorer's table, and by the time I get back to the huddle Coach is already giving instructions.

"If they stay in their zone, just move the ball around and look for the first open shot. Don't be afraid to take it. Just like the two-minute drill. Square up and shoot it. Then crash the boards."

Coach grabs a clipboard and a marker and draws a play. He points to the diagram.

"If they switch to man-to-man defense, Bryce, you set a pick for Davonn on the left side. Davonn, cut to the basket. If you're not open, get it out to Richie on the right wing for the shot. Let's do it!"

I can hardly feel my feet as we step back onto the court. Grady dribbles downcourt. The clock clicks off the remaining seconds. "They're in man-to-man!" Grady shouts. "Set it up!"

Davonn swings over to the left side as I set up near the right corner. Bryce sets the pick on the left side.

Time is running out...11...10...9...

Grady passes the ball to Davonn.

Davonn fakes left and drives right around Bryce's pick.

The Saratoga center moves over to cut off Davonn from the basket. Davonn has no shot so he tosses the ball to me on the right side.

The crowd is chanting now, "Three... two..."

I know I have to shoot right away. There's no time to think or be nervous. The ball is in the air a split second after it touches my hands. The buzzer sounds as the ball flies through the air.

It feels like everyone in the gym—the coaches, the players, the people in the stands—is holding their breath as the ball arcs down, wondering whether the shot will be good.

But the shooter already knows.

Swish!

CHAPTER 9

I know Christmas comes the same time every year, and I'm usually happy for the break. But after hitting the winning basket against Saratoga, all I want to do is keep practicing my shooting and playing hoops.

After the Saratoga game, Coach Sheridan announces that we won't practice again until January second. That's a long time without basketball.

"You can still work out on your own," he tells us. "Run, shoot around, play pickup. Anything to stay in shape."

That's fine, but Coach doesn't figure on the big snowstorm that hits right after school ends for the holiday break. Eight to ten inches cover the town. There's no way for

Bryce and me to run in Stone Creek Park or shoot hoops outside with all that snow. It's even too cold and wintery for us to shoot around in my driveway.

We get a workout—and make some money—shoveling snow. But after doing a couple of driveways Bryce gets a blister on his hand.

"I need these hands for rebounding," he says.

I feel the same way. "Yeah. And I need mine for shooting."

Of course, the snow makes my mom happy. She takes a week off from work around Christmas. She and Jeanie spend the week singing Christmas songs and doing more of our family's one million Christmas traditions.

My dad the English professor started us out reading Christmas stories together when we were little kids, stories like *A Christmas Carol* by Charles Dickens and *A Christmas Memory* by Truman Capote.

The second one is my favorite. It's about a little kid living down South years ago who makes fruitcakes every Christmas with his crazy old cousin. I know it doesn't sound that great, but it's really cool to read aloud.

It gets so hectic with holiday stuff around our house that I'm kind of glad when Christmas is finally over. It's cold and we get more snow two days later.

I'm so anxious to get back in the swing of things that I think about shoveling the court down at the playground. But that won't do anything about the freezing temperatures. There's no way to play hoops outside.

I can almost feel my shooting touch slipping away over the holiday. I hit the game winner against Saratoga, but I missed a lot of shots too. Madison told me I was two for seven from the floor—Cammy wouldn't show me the stats. Two for seven. That's just 28 percent. Not so great. I need to work on my shot.

So I call Bryce on the Friday morning after Christmas. "We've got to find a way to get into the school gym," I say.

"I'm game, but how are we going to do it?"

"Why don't we grab a ball and go down

to the school," I suggest. "Maybe Mr. Garcia will let us in."

"He's just the janitor," Bryce says. "He's not going to let a couple of kids roam around the school over Christmas break."

"He's a good guy. Maybe he'll let us in if we promise him we'll stay around the gym. It's worth a try. I mean, we're not doing anything now."

So Bryce and I trudge along the frozen streets to school.

As we approach the parking lot, I spot Mr. Garcia's truck. I know it's his because of the Green Bay Packers bumper sticker. He's a huge Packers fan.

"He's got to be here," I tell Bryce.

We look into a couple of windows near the front of the school and try the doors. No luck.

Bryce and I circle around to the gym door. We stand there for a moment, each wondering the same thing.

"Go ahead, try it," Bryce says.

I pull at the door handle. It opens!

We step out onto the court. It's funny to be in the gym when no one is around. It's quiet, almost like a church. And cold too. Not as cold as outside, but definitely chilly. We start to pass the ball back and forth to warm up. Bryce sends me a bounce pass. The ball slapping against the gym floor sounds so loud! The noise echoes against the gym walls.

Finally I take a shot. The ball bounces off the rim.

"I'm rusty."

"Keep shooting," Bryce says. "You'll get your touch back."

I take some more shots. More misses.

"C'mon, let me have a try." Bryce makes a few and misses a few. His shooting doesn't seem any different than before the break.

I float toward the three-point line and hold out my hands. "Give me the ball."

More misses. I get this panicky feeling in my stomach. It's like my shot disappeared over the break like a box of Christmas candy.

"Hey, what are you doing here?" a voice asks from the other end of the gym.

I turn and see Cammy standing with her hands on her hips. I'm relieved it's not Mr. Garcia.

60

"What am *I* doing here? What are *you* doing here?" I ask.

"I'm helping out my dad today."

I think for a moment. "Oh, I didn't know Mr. Garcia was your dad."

"You never asked."

"We're just shooting around," Bryce explains. "Is that okay?"

"You know you're not supposed to be here." She gives us a look, then adds, "But I'll find out if it's okay with my dad."

I glance over at Bryce.

"Don't worry," Cammy says. "I'll put in a good word for you."

I keep trying, but my shot doesn't come back by the time Cammy returns.

"My dad says it's okay but that I should stay down here just to keep an eye on you." She grabs a book from her backpack and sits down in the corner.

Bryce and I take turns shooting. A couple of shots fall in, but it seems like luck. Sure enough, I go cold again. Nothing's going in. The ball feels heavy and strange in my hands. I can feel my heart speeding up in my chest.

After about twenty minutes, Bryce checks his phone. "Hey, I've got to go," he says.

"Come on, stick around. I want to shoot more. I still don't have my shot back."

Bryce shakes his head. "My mom just texted me. She wants me home. Now." He heads for the door.

"Okay, I'll see you later. I'm going to stay a while longer. Is that okay, Cammy?"

She sets down her book. "I'll rebound for you."

I have my doubts. I've hardly seen Cammy touch a basketball except to put them away after practice. But what choice do I have? I need to practice my shot, and shooting alone is hard. "Okay, thanks," I say.

Turns out Cammy is a pretty good rebounder. Not as good as Bryce, but close.

"I thought you didn't play hoops," I say after another miss.

"I don't. I play soccer and lacrosse."

Another shot circles the rim and rattles out. "Come on!" I shout. "That was in!"

Cammy grabs the rebound and holds the ball.

"What are you doing?" I ask. "I thought you were rebounding. Give me the ball."

"You think a lot about your shot, don't you?"

"Yeah, so what? I'm the shooter."

"So there are other parts of the game, you know, like rebounding, passing, playing defense."

"I thought you played lacrosse."

"It's the same in lacrosse, except rebounding is called getting loose balls."

"I do all that other stuff," I insist.

Cammy looks at me like she doesn't believe me. "Don't forget, I keep the stats," she says. "I don't remember marking down many rebounds and assists for you. I don't think I put down a single one in the first two games."

I look at Cammy without saying anything. My neck is getting warm even though it's about 60 degrees in the gym. I'm mad at Cammy, the snow, and all my misses.

"I'm just saying," she says.

"Well, why don't you just rebound?" I snap.

Bad move. It's like something flares up in

Cammy's eyes. She doesn't say a word. She bounces me the ball, turns on her heel, and picks up her book off the floor. She walks away without looking back.

I want to call out—say that I'm sorry. But it's too late. She's gone.

I take another shot. I miss.

CHAPTER 10

My shot is gone. Disappeared. It's floated away like one of those helium balloons when you let go of the string. Lost.

I was hoping it would show up when we got back from the break and started practicing again. No such luck.

I'm not missing *every* shot. Nobody does that. But I never seem to get hot like I used to. Even worse, when I let go of the ball, I don't believe the shots are going in. It's like I'm not the shooter anymore. It's like I'm not *me* anymore.

I tell Cammy I'm sorry about snapping at her during the rebounding thing in the gym. She says it's no big deal. I'm not sure she really means it, but I'm not going there. If she says things are okay between us that's fine with me.

Maybe things *are* okay, because she shows me the stats for the two-minute drill at the end of the last practice before the Fair Hill game.

Sure enough, my numbers are going down. Even worse, C. J.'s numbers are creeping up.

"Try passing and rebounding more," Cammy tells me.

Somehow her advice doesn't sit right with me. It's like she's feeling sorry for me or something. I'm the shooter. I've got to shoot. Since when does Cammy know so much about hoops anyway? She's a lacrosse player.

Still, part of me wants to show Cammy that I can do more than shoot. So before the Fair Hill game I promise myself I'll grab at least one rebound and dish out one assist.

The Fair Hill Falcons are good, even better than Saratoga. They're tough on defense and unselfish on offense. We fall behind quickly, 12–6.

Coach puts me in early. "We need some

offense," he says. "Look for your shot."

Jeez, what does he think I've been doing since before the Christmas break? I kneel at the scorer's table waiting to get in. I'd better find my shot, fast.

The Falcons are on me quick. The Fair Hill coach stands up the moment I come in the game and shouts, "Ethan, you got the new guy!"

The kid Ethan is all over me. He's got arms and legs that are so long it's like Spider-Man is covering me. I can hardly get an open look.

Davonn gets me the ball on the wing, my favorite spot. I fake a shot and Spider-Man falls for it. I drive to the basket and slip a sweet bounce pass to Mason, who lays the ball off the glass and in.

Mason points at me as we run downcourt. "Nice pass," Bryce chimes in. I glance over at Cammy. She's marking the play down in the scorebook. An assist. Maybe that will keep her quiet for a while.

Fair Hill takes a shot that bounces out past the foul line. I grab the rebound and turn to look at Grady. He catches the Fair Hill defense by surprise and streaks downcourt several steps ahead of everyone. I toss a long chest pass that lands in front of him, and he gathers it in and sprints in for the layup.

A rebound and another assist. That should definitely shut Cammy up.

Our comeback doesn't last long. The Falcons grab back the lead. I don't help much. I force up a couple of shots, but they clang off the rim and fall away. We trail by five at halftime, 26–21, and I don't have a point.

Coach tries to get us back on track with a halftime pep talk. "Move the ball around. Make the extra pass. Make them work on defense. When you get the open shot, take it. The shots will start falling for us."

He's talking to me, I think.

We're all trying, but nothing works. We slip farther behind in the second half. I grab another rebound and pass off to Davonn for a bucket. That makes two rebounds and three assists. But Spider-Man is all over me and I don't make a shot—not a single bucket—the whole game.

We fall so far behind that Coach puts in the end-of-the-bench players for the last two minutes of the game. I sit on the bench as the final few seconds of the game tick away. I look at the scoreboard and shake my head.

VISITOR   KNIGHTS

53   0:22   QTR 4   36

"They're good," I whisper to Bryce.

"We can beat them." Bryce slaps his towel against the floor. "We just didn't play very well."

I stare out as Scott scores one last meaningless basket. "You mean *I* didn't play very well."

"You played okay. You just didn't hit your shot."

Just didn't hit my shot, I think. *That's like saying a sprinter didn't run very fast.*

The buzzer sounds and we walk slowly toward the locker room door.

"Hey, Madison," Bryce says. "Can I take a look at the stats?"

She tilts the book toward him. I look over his shoulder.

"Tough game," says Madison.

Cammy's busy gathering up her stuff and doesn't look at me.

Player	FGs	FTs	Rebs	Assists	Points
Davonn Peters	4/10	2/2	4	2	10
Bryce Cooper	1/4	1/2	5	1	3
Mason Gregg	2/6	2/2	6	0	6
Charles Jackson	1/5	1/2	2	2	3
Grady Lin	2/5	0/2	0	2	4
Richie Mallon	0/5	0/0	2	3	0
Theo Kirshner	1/2	0/0	1	0	2
Anthony Delgado	2/4	0/0	2	0	4
Quinton McDaniel	0/0	0/0	1	0	0
Ray Burns	1/3	0/2	0	1	2
Scott Hamilton	1/1	0/0	1	0	2
Totals:	**15/45**	**6/12**	**24**	**11**	**36**

3-point goals: None

"Hey, Richie," says Madison. "Nice job with the rebounds and assists."

But the only number I can see on the stat sheet is a big zero. Zero for five.

Zero points for me. The shooter.

CHAPTER 11

The next few games are more of the same. It's not like I'm putting up zeroes every game, but I'm not lighting it up either.

It's funny. At the beginning of the season I decided to track my own game statistics. I thought it would be a record of all my great shooting games. But after the first game, the numbers seem to be laughing at me.

Opponent	FGs	FGA	FTs	Points
Burr	4	5	1/2	9
Saratoga	2	7	0/0	4
Fair Hill	0	5	0/0	0
Culbert	1	4	2/2	4
Stone Mill	2	6	1/2	5
Burr	1	5	1/2	3

And the pathetic numbers aren't my only problem. When things are going badly with basketball, I have no one to talk to about it at home. If my parents are home, my dad always has his head in a book and my mom is usually thinking about her patients.

To make things worse, Jeanie got a big part in the school musical. She's Marian the librarian in *The Music Man*, so she goes around the house singing "Good Night My Someone" and "Till There Was You" all the time. It's driving me crazy.

Anyway, it seems like Mom and Dad are a lot more into Jeanie being Marian the librarian than they are into me being the shooter. I don't think they even know I'm in a shooting slump. I'm not sure they even know what a shooting slump is.

I know missing a few shots isn't such a big deal next to writing about Shakespeare or helping sick kids or even starring in a musical. But it's a big deal to me.

One Saturday in early February I call Bryce. It's still too cold and windy to shoot outside. I suggest going down to the school so I can work on my shot.

"Maybe Mr. Garcia will let us in again," I say.

"I can't."

"Why not?"

"I've got to watch my little brother. My parents are out."

"Bring him."

"I can't. He's autistic, remember? He doesn't do real well in new places. He kind of likes to have his own stuff around."

"Okay, then. See you Monday," I say and hang up.

I walk down to the school, bouncing the ball through the gray winter weather. The first block I dribble with my right hand. The next I use my left. I practice dribbling between my legs whenever I wait at a corner.

Mr. Garcia's truck is in the parking lot again, so I walk straight up to the gym door.

It's locked, so I knock two or three times. When no one answers, I start wondering if I should just leave. What if Cammy is here and starts in on that work-on-your-other-skills stuff again? I turn away, but then I hear a voice.

"Okay, okay! Hold on, I'm coming. Don't break the door down."

The door swings open. Cammy's standing there with one of those wide floor mops in her hand.

"You again." She spots the basketball under my arm. "You here to work on your shot?"

"If I can, that would be great." I step in out of the winter weather and blow on my cold hands.

Cammy looks around as if she's making sure no one is watching. "I guess it's okay. But first I have to finish sweeping the floor."

"You helping your dad again?"

She nods and points to the wall. "Wait on the side over there."

"Need any help?"

"I'm okay. Anyway, there's only one mop."

I sit down on the basketball and lean against the wall. I watch Cammy walk up and down the gym floor pushing the wide mop in front of her.

"You always help your dad?"

"He's got me on Wednesdays and weekends." She turns to start another row. "My parents are divorced."

"Sorry."

"Don't be. It wasn't so great when they were married." She makes another turn and continues. "I hang out here on Saturdays. Do my homework. Help out a little bit. Keep my dad company."

She makes a final pass and pushes the dust and dirt into a little pile. "There you go," she says. "It's perfect. Just for you."

I start warming up. Dribbling, shooting, just getting the feel of the ball and the floor. Cammy sweeps up the dirt from the corner and puts it in a big gray plastic barrel.

"Want me to rebound for you again?" she asks.

"Sure. I mean if you can. Don't you need to help your dad?"

She shakes her head. "I did the floor. Rebounding for you beats doing math homework."

I'm still kind of wondering if she's mad at me about the last time she rebounded so I say, "Thanks for rebounding. It helps me a lot."

"No worries. Come on, start shooting."

I get down to the serious stuff of working on my shot. I settle into a rhythm and for the first time in I don't know how long the shots start dropping in.

Cammy counts the baskets. "Three... four...five...six..."

The next shot rolls off the rim.

"Start over," I say.

"One..."

I miss the next one, thudding the ball off the rim. "Again." My voice is getting a little too loud.

This time I miss the very first shot. Cammy hustles after the ball. She puts it on her hip and walks back slowly.

"You've been getting a lot more rebounds and assists lately," she says.

"Yeah, but I'm still shooting lousy."

"Name a great shooter," she says.

"What are you talking about? Why?"

"Go ahead, name one."

"All right, Steph Curry. He's the best."

Cammy smiles like she figured that's what I would say. "Okay, but he's also a great point guard, ball handler, passer, and team leader. He plays decent defense too. Lot of steals. Who else?"

"James Harden."

"Yeah, he's a beast. But he doesn't just shoot the ball. He gets a boatload of assists. Especially for a shooting guard."

"How do you know so much about hoops?" I ask. "I thought you were into lacrosse."

"I watch a lot of sports with my dad. Name another shooter."

"Okay, okay. I get your point. Give me the ball."

Cammy isn't listening. She just keeps talking. "Your shot will come around," she says. "And when it does, you'll be awesome. Until then, keep rebounding, passing, and playing defense. Just keep playing the game."

She fakes me a pass and I instinctively put out my hands for the ball. I really want to keep shooting.

She holds onto the ball and gives me a little smile. "I'm just saying."

CHAPTER 12

Maybe it's because of what Cammy said yesterday, but I'm feeling restless. It's Sunday morning and there isn't much to do. It's my mom's one day off, so she and my dad hang around the family room reading the papers and listening to classical music. Jeanie is singing somewhere in the house.

I've checked all my favorite basketball websites. The sun is out and the day is not too cold—maybe in the high 40s—and all the Christmas snow is gone.

I give Bryce a call before noon. "You want to go for a run at Stone Creek Park?"

He sounds less than enthusiastic. "Don't

we run enough at basketball practice?"

"We won't run that hard. Just a jog to stay loose. Come on, it's a nice day. I want to get out of the house and do something. I'm tired of listening to Vivaldi."

"Who?"

"Never mind. What do you say?"

"Okay. I'll meet you at the park in fifteen minutes."

I get to the park first and stand around waiting, pacing near the entrance to the trail. The bright sun makes the bare tree branches look like they're lit in high-def.

Bryce arrives, looking like he's still sleepy. "Remember, you said we're not running that hard."

"Stop being such a whiner," I say. "We won't run that hard, I promise. Why are you so tired?"

"Hey, I'm under the boards all the time, remember?" Bryce says with an edge in his voice. "Getting rebounds, setting picks for guys like you. Doing the dirty work. You just hang around outside looking for your shot."

"Okay, okay," I say as we enter the park

and pick up the trail. "We'll take it slow...for Mr. Whiny-Pants."

We start off at a slow jog, picking our way carefully past the exposed rocks. It's quiet along the creek. Most of the birds are gone, spending the winter in a warmer place. The trail is sunnier than in the summer or fall because the leaves are off the tree branches and on the ground.

"Did you go over to the school yesterday?" Bryce asks as we ramp up the pace.

"Yeah."

"Did you get in?"

"Yeah, Cammy let me in. She even rebounded for me again."

"I didn't know she played hoop."

"She doesn't. But she's a good athlete. She plays soccer and lacrosse." I glance over at Bryce. His breath sends puffs of smoke into the cold air. "And after all, it's not so hard to be a rebounder," I tease.

"You don't think rebounding is hard?" I can hear the edge in Bryce's voice again. "Maybe you should try it sometime."

Ouch. I figure I'd better cool things off,

fast. "Hey, come on. I was only joking around. You don't have to get all bent out of shape."

Bryce stares straight ahead like he doesn't even want to look at me. "All I'm saying is if you think rebounding is so easy, then come on underneath the boards and try it. Mason and I could use the help." He glances over and then looks quickly away. "How many rebounds have you got this season?"

"I got a few against Fair Hill."

"Oh wow. Call Sports Center."

I have to admit, that one stings. Mostly because, as Cammy pointed out, I don't have a lot of rebounds on my stat sheet.

"All right. All right." We fall back into our jogging pace, running in silence as we make our way up the hill.

"My shot started coming back a little bit," I say, thinking I'm changing the subject.

"You think about your shot too much," Bryce snaps. "Just play the game."

"That's the same thing Cammy told me." I feel like I'm making a confession.

"That girl's smart," Bryce says. "She keeps the stats. She knows what's up."

Bryce and I run in an awkward silence for what seems to be a long time. We're on the easy part of the trail. We pass an older woman walking an even older dog.

In the silence I begin to feel sorry for myself. Angry thoughts bounce around in my head. *Everybody—Bryce, Cammy, even the lady at the Christmas tree farm—seems to be ganging up on me.*

We take a corner and jog past a series of fallen tree trunks that have been sawed into large pieces and moved to the side of the trail.

I'm the shooter. I have been since I started playing hoops in the driveway. I bet everyone wouldn't be talking like this if I was hitting my shots. Nobody was talking about rebounds and assists when I hit the game winner against Saratoga. I almost wish I hadn't asked Bryce to come for a run. It would've been better to be out here by myself.

"How do you think we'll do against Saratoga this week?" Bryce asks, breaking the long silence. I can sense he's trying for a truce. Maybe he feels bad about coming down so hard on me about my shot and my not rebounding.

"We should do okay," I say. "After all, we beat them last time."

We're at the road that cuts through the park. Almost done. We jog in place as a few cars go by. I keep thinking about what everyone has been saying. Tossing it over in my mind.

Just play the game. Don't think so much about your shot. Get some rebounds. Pass the ball. Hand out some assists. Your shot will come around.

We jog across the street after the last car whizzes by.

Then it hits me.

Maybe Bryce, Cammy, and the Christmas tree lady aren't ganging up on me. Maybe they're right.

CHAPTER 13

Tweeeeeeeet! Coach Sheridan blows his whistle. I'm surprised that whistle still works. Seems like it would be worn out by now.

"All right, let's scrimmage."

Those words are music to my ears. At last we can stop doing the orange cone drill. We're more than halfway through the season and I still can't stand those cones.

Of course, scrimmaging isn't so great either, since I'm stuck on the second team— the Blue shirts. I think Coach has stopped thinking of me as a possible starter, and I can't blame him. A shooter who isn't shooting so great can't start for anyone.

"Let's play man-to-man defense today," Coach says, walking toward the middle of the court. "Remember, against the man-to-man, the idea is to pass and pick away from the ball. Keep moving and cutting through the middle."

Coach points to the scorer's table. "Game to twenty. I'll referee. Cammy and Madison, keep the score and the stats just like it was a real game."

Great. Make it official that the White shirts beat the Blue shirts for the hundred millionth time in a row. The Blues haven't won a scrimmage all year. Maybe that's why Bryce thinks he can tell me to "just play the game." He's always on the first team—the White shirts.

I circle up with Anthony, Ray, Quinton, and Link. "I'm covering Bryce," Anthony says. The others quickly choose who they want to cover.

"Looks like you've got Davonn," Ray says to me with a crooked little smile.

I glare at him. "Thanks for nothing."

Davonn is brutal to cover. He's skinny, but

strong and super quick. He has a whole lot of ways to score...and to make you look stupid on defense.

Sure enough, the Whites score a couple of quick buckets. They start slapping backs, feeling good and talking trash. Madison puts the numbers up on the electronic scoreboard. Cammy marks down everything in the scorebook. Just like in a real game.

On offense, I try looking for my shot. But Davonn's all over me. He's serious about defense today. The other guys are watching me too. They know the only way they're going to lose is if I get hot and start making baskets.

I drive to the hoop and draw the defense, then pass it back to Ray near the foul line. He's not a great shooter, but...

Swish! The score is 4–2. At least we're on the board.

I grab a long rebound after a missed shot and start a fast break. I dribble to the middle and dish off to Quinton, who hustles downcourt for the layup. Up and in. It's 4–4.

Davonn forces up a shot and Link grabs

the rebound. We're off and running again. After a series of quick passes, Anthony lays it in. Now we're up, 6–4. The Blues are feeling a whole lot better.

We trade baskets, still holding on to a slim lead, 12–10. The Blues are playing well. We're moving the ball, setting picks, playing defense. Just like Coach told us. Still, the Whites don't seem really worried.

I get the ball in my favorite spot—the left wing. But instead of letting one fly, I look inside and see Link with his hand raised. I slip a quick entry pass to the tall seventh grader, who flips a sweet little baby hook shot off the glass and in, pushing the score to 14–10.

Now Davonn, Bryce, and the rest of the Whites are getting rattled. They start yelling at each other instead of talking trash to us.

"Come on!" Davonn shouts as the Whites come downcourt. "Let's play some D!"

"Yeah!" Bryce barks. "Tighten it up."

Hustling back on defense, I start thinking Davonn's going to try to be the hero. He gets the ball on the wing. I guess he'll drive right and so I step in front. Sure enough, Davonn plows right into me. We tumble to the hardwood.

Tweeeeeeeet!

Coach Sheridan puts his hand in back of his head. "Charge, offensive foul, Blue ball," he calls, pointing our way. Davonn slams the ball down and runs back on defense.

I get the ball on the wing. I fake a shot and Davonn jumps to block it. I dribble by him and then dish off to Link for an easy two. We're ahead 16–10.

The Whites get really serious looks in their eyes—like they want to teach us a lesson. Bryce hits a short jumper. Davonn drives past me for a layup. Mason scores on a putback. In no time it's tied, 16–16.

Coach Sheridan puts a little pressure on everybody. "Losers have to run sprints."

Ray drives and passes to me at the three-point line. My shot's a little long and bounces off the back of the rim. But I follow the shot and tip the rebound inside to Link, who lays the ball up and in. We're up 18–16. That's a big hoop.

The Blues are completely psyched now. We can almost taste a win. We run back on defense, yelling.

"Come on, play D! We can beat these guys!"

"Tighten it up! Don't give them anything easy!"

"We just need one more basket! One more."

Grady gets Davonn the ball. He fakes right and spins left. I stay with him the best I can and force him to throw up an off-balanced shot that bounces off the rim.

Link snags the rebound and flips a quick pass to me on the side. I look downcourt and spy Ray streaking down the middle. It's worth a try. I hook a long pass that Ray grabs, beating C. J. by a step. He spins the ball off the backboard and it slips through the net.

The Blues win, 20–16, in what feels like the sweetest win of the year.

"All right, first team!" Coach Sheridan shouts. "Give me five."

The Blues stand along the sidelines. We're slapping backs and yelling at the poor Whites running sprints up and down the court.

"Come on, hustle!"

"Get the lead out!"

"Move it! Move it!"

I can't help but laugh watching those guys drag their tired butts up and down the court. I'm so glad it's not us again. Even though the Whites will probably kill us the next time we scrimmage, and even though I didn't score a single point during the Blues win, I'm still really psyched about our victory.

I start walking out. "Want to see the stats?" Cammy asks.

"Not much to see," I say, not sure what Cammy's up to. "I didn't score a point."

Cammy shakes her head as if I'm crazy. "Take a look."

WHITES

	FGs	FTs	Rebs	Assists	Points
Davonn Peters	2/7	0/0	3	1	4
Bryce Cooper	2/4	0/0	5	1	4
Mason Gregg	2/5	0/0	5	0	4
Charles Jackson	1/3	0/0	2	1	2
Grady Lin	1/3	0/0	0	1	2
Totals	**8/22**	**0/0**	**15**	**4**	**16**

BLUES

	FGs	FTs	Rebs	Assists	Points
Richie Mallon	0/2	0/0	3	5	0
Lincoln Jones	5/8	0/0	4	0	10
Anthony Delgado	2/4	0/0	3	1	4
Quinton McDaniel	1/3	0/0	2	0	2
Ray Burns	2/3	0/0	1	1	4
Totals	**10/20**	**0/0**	**13**	**7**	**20**

"You probably played the best twenty minutes you've played all year. Five assists. Three rebounds. You did a really good job on Davonn. Oh yeah, and one more thing...you guys won."

I look at the stats. Cammy's right. I filled up all the columns except scoring. And Davonn only scored four points. I glance up.

Cammy's smiling. "I'm—"

I hold up my hand to stop her. "I know, I know. You're just saying."

CHAPTER 14

Warm-ups before the game against Saratoga start with the usual Sheridan layup drills. Balls buzz around and everybody twists toward the basket. I start getting the feel for the ball and the speed of the game. It's great to hear my teammates clapping their hands and shouting so loud their voices bounce off the walls.

"Let's go, Knights!"

"Let's get it done!"

"Everybody scores today!"

All the noise and energy makes me feel like I could jump right out of the building.

But then comes the part that I don't like. Coach Sheridan always has us end warm-ups with a loose shoot-around. Everyone starts shooting at the same time. Ten basketballs fly toward the bucket and knock each other around like bumper cars when they get near the rim. Half the time the ball I shoot bangs into another shot and I can't tell if *my* shot was any good or not.

So just before every game when the referee blows the whistle for play to begin and the rest of the team goes to huddle with Coach, I sneak one last outside shot while the coast is clear.

Today's shot drops right through the bucket. Nothing but net. That's a good sign. Maybe, just maybe, my shot is back.

Coach gives his usual final instructions before the game. By this point in the season I think everyone could recite them word for word.

"Move the ball. Talk on defense. Hustle. Work for a good shot. Everybody help out on the boards."

When I head toward the bench with the rest of the Blues, Coach motions for Link and me to stay close.

"I may put you guys in a little sooner today," he says, patting the bench beside him.

I like the sound of that.

Sure enough, three minutes into the game Link and I are kneeling at the scorer's table waiting to get in. I glance at the scoreboard.

We're behind 10–6. I elbow Link. "Move around under the basket like you did in the scrimmage the other day," I say. "I'll try to get you the ball. If it worked against the Whites, it ought to work against Saratoga."

Link and I light the spark. I get the ball on the wing and snap an entry pass in to Link, who puts a quick move on the Saratoga center. Up and in. Two points.

"That's my baby!" Link's mother is up,

waving her cane and shouting from the first row of the stands. Link is right. That lady has a voice on her.

The team starts clicking. We turn up the defensive pressure. Hands up, tipping passes, making life miserable for the Saratoga guys.

Grady darts out and steals a pass. We're off to the races. It's two-on-one and just like in practice, Grady and I pass the ball back and forth, spinning the defender's head around until I lay the ball off the backboard and into the basket.

The Saratoga coach is up off the bench calling a timeout. We've come back and are up 16–12.

Coach Sheridan is up too. "Ray, report in for Grady. Let's keep the pressure on."

"That's three Blues," I whisper to Bryce.

"I don't care what shirts you wear as long as you guys keep playing well," he says as we break the huddle.

The Blues (along with Davonn and Bryce) keep it going with ball-hawking defense and fast-breaking offense.

I'm trailing a fast break when Davonn

passes the ball out to me beyond the three-point line. I haven't been shooting well, but I'm open and it feels good.

Swish!

"Yes!" I shout and pump a fist.

A few minutes later I get the ball on the right wing. I whip a pass in to Davonn, who's cutting to the basket. He takes it up strong.

Tweeeeeeeeet! The referee blows his whistle as the ball slips through the net. "The basket is good. Foul on number 5."

I glance over to the scorer's table, knowing that Cammy is marking down everything.

Coach leaves me in almost the entire first half. We're ahead 28–17 at halftime.

The second half is more of the same. Coach puts me in early and our team keeps running, scoring, and playing defense.

I grab some rebounds and start some fast breaks that end in layups. I miss a couple of long shots, but I make a few. I have my share of passes too.

Link is having a big game underneath. I figure he's going to be scrimmaging with the Whites pretty soon.

We run away with an easy win. The final score is 53–31. Everyone's exhausted from cheering so much.

I stop at the scorer's table. "Did we keep you busy enough?" I ask Cammy.

She smiles. "I think I got it all. Want to take a look to be sure?"

I study the stats.

PLAYER	FGs	FTs	Rebs	Assists	Points
Davonn Peters	5/9	2/2	5	3	12
Bryce Cooper	2/4	2/4	5	2	6
Mason Gregg	2/6	2/2	5	0	6
Charles Jackson	1/2	0/0	2	2	2
Grady Lin	2/5	1/2	0	2	5
Richie Mallon	3/5	2/2	4	3	9
Lincoln Jones	4/6	0/0	1	0	8
Anthony Delgado	2/4	0/0	2	0	4
Quinton McDaniel	0/1	0/0	2	0	0
Ray Burns	0/2	1/2	0	2	1
Totals:	**21/44**	**10/14**	**26**	**14**	**53**

3-point goals: Mallon (1)

Sensing how pumped I am about the game, Cammy says, "Nine points, three assists, and four rebounds—oh, and don't forget the steal. You did a little bit of everything today. And your shot seems to be coming back."

"*Seems* to be coming back? Hey, I'm still the shooter," I say, pretending to be hurt. But I'm too happy to keep joking around. I point at the stat sheet again. "Did you get all of Link's points and rebounds? He was awesome."

"I think so," she says. "Although it *was* hard to keep up." She tilts her head toward the row where Link's mother had been sitting. "I just listened for his mom. Any time she yelled, 'That's my boy!' I knew I had to write something in the book for him."

"Yeah," I agree with a laugh. "She walked in here leaning on a cane, but I think she left dancing."

CHAPTER 15

I walk through the front door with my backpack slung over my right shoulder.

"Hello, hello, hello!" I shout to see if anyone else is around.

"Hey, Richie!" my dad yells from the kitchen. "In here!"

I walk back. I can hear Jeanie upstairs singing "Till There Was You" for the hundred millionth time. My dad is chopping vegetables at the cutting board. I grab a carrot.

"How was school today?" he asks without looking up from the cutting board.

"We played Saratoga."

Dad stops chopping and gives me a disappointed look. "Really? If you'd told me, I might have gone to the game. I didn't have any classes this afternoon."

"Come on, Dad. The schedule's been on the refrigerator for a couple of months. We play just about every Thursday." I grab a pen and go over and mark the score down on the schedule.

PLAZA MIDDLE SCHOOL KNIGHTS— BOYS BASKETBALL

Date	Opponent	Time	
December 7	Burr MS	4 p.m	W 46–40
December 14	@ Saratoga MS	4 p.m.	W 43–42
January 4	Fair Hill MS	4 p.m.	L 53–36
January 11	@ Culbert MS	4 p.m.	W 48–41
January 18	Stone Mill MS	4 p.m.	W 55–29
January 25	@ Burr MS	4 p.m.	W 42–38
February 1	Saratoga MS	4 p.m.	W 53–31
February 8	@ Fair Hill MS	4 p.m.	
February 15	Culbert MS	4 p.m.	
February 22	@ Stone Mill MS	4 p.m.	

I open the fridge to look inside. Everything looks a little too healthy to eat after a big win.

Dad goes back to chopping veggies. "I'm really sorry I forgot about the game."

"That's okay."

It is okay. I'm not just saying it to make him feel better. I know some kids' parents come to every game. Bryce's mom and dad? They wouldn't miss a game if their house was on fire. My parents aren't really into sports. It's just the way they are. Like having blue eyes or something. Anyway, I know they care about me. They know I love playing hoops. They don't have to come to every game to prove it. It's no big deal.

Dad squints down at a recipe card. "Well, how was the game?" he asks.

I point to the schedule on the refrigerator. "We won 53–31."

"Really? Sounds like I missed a good one."

"Yeah, we played great. What're we having tonight?"

"Curried chicken with veggies over basmati rice."

"When will we eat?"

Dad checks the clock on the stove. "Around 6:30."

"Where's Mom?"

"Still at the office. She said she should be home by 6:30, but that if she isn't we should start without her."

Jeanie walks in. She's still singing "Till There Was You." She belts it out, like she's onstage and singing to the back row.

"Can you hit the shuffle button on your playlist?" I ask. "You've been singing the same song for weeks."

An annoyed look sweeps across Jeanie's face. "I've got to practice," she says. "The first show is in less than two weeks. Anyway, what would you want me to sing?"

"I don't know...how about 'Call Me Maybe.'"

"Omigosh, Richie. You are so totally out of it. That was popular a million years ago!"

She's got me there—I don't know a lot about music. But I'll give Jeanie credit. She switches to the old Carly Rae Jepsen song without skipping a beat. Complete with the hand motions like she's talking on the phone. She even picks up a spoon and pretends it's a microphone.

I mean, she's so good that I start dancing

around with her...a little bit. I'm not a great dancer.

"You should sing that song in the show," I say.

Dad laughs. "I don't think Marian the librarian would sing 'Call Me Maybe.'"

Jeanie suddenly gets all serious. "She might. She really likes Harold Hill—the music man—but she's kind of shy so—"

"So Marian sings 'Call Me Maybe'?" Dad makes a face like there's no way that would happen. "I don't think so."

I laugh. "I'll give you five bucks if you sing it for real in the show."

Jeanie shakes her head. "You'll have to pay me way more than that, little brother, for me to make a complete fool of myself in front of the whole school...and all the parents."

"Okay, ten bucks."

"All right, all right," Dad says, holding up his hands. "You guys have forty-five minutes before dinner. You can go upstairs and get some homework done and I'll call you when dinner's ready, or you can stay here and help me with the cooking."

Jeannie walks out still singing "Call Me Maybe."

So what if I don't keep up with the latest pop songs. At least I got her to shuffle her playlist.

I head upstairs and toss my backpack on my bed. I take out my laptop and click around until I get to my list of shooting stats for the year.

Opponent	FGs	FGA	FTs	Points
Burr	4	5	1/2	9
Saratoga	2	7	0/0	4
Fair Hill	0	5	0/0	0
Culbert	1	4	2/2	4
Stone Mill	2	6	1/2	5
Burr	1	5	1/2	3
Saratoga	3	5	2/2	9
Fair Hill				
Culbert				
Stone Mill				

I type in the score of the Saratoga game and my shots and my points. I look at the list. Something's missing. I type in the rebounds and the assists too.

Opponent	FGs	FGA	FTs	Points	Rebs	Assists
Saratoga	3	5	2/2	9	3	4

That's better. Now I can fill in all the columns.

CHAPTER 16

I'm lacing up my sneakers in the locker room for practice when Bryce bangs open the doors.

"Where's Coach Sheridan?"

"What are you talking about? Isn't he upstairs in the gym?"

"I didn't see him."

"That's weird. He's always upstairs waiting for us."

Davonn laughs. "If he's late for practice, can we make him run wind sprints?"

"I wouldn't count on it."

The team wanders into the gym. No Coach Sheridan. A couple of guys grab basketballs and start to dribble and shoot around.

I notice Cammy at the scorer's table. "Hey, Cammy!" I shout. "Have you seen Coach Sheridan?"

She shakes her head. "No, I figured he was down in the locker room with you guys."

I look at the clock. It's 3:30. Time for practice to start. Some more guys grab balls and start shooting.

"What are we going to do?" I ask Bryce, Davonn, and some of the eighth graders.

"Layups?" Bryce suggests with a shrug of his shoulders.

"Let's do it," Davonn agrees. "Just so long as we don't do the orange cone drill. Man, I hate that one."

Bryce and Davonn take charge. After all, they're starters and eighth graders. "Let's go!" they shout. "Layup drills."

We fall in just as if Coach Sheridan had blown his whistle. In a few seconds players and balls are whipping around the floor at game-time speed.

"Count 'em!" Bryce yells as another shot touches off the backboard and slips through the net.

"Five...six...seven...eight...." We aren't missing.

The team finishes layups and starts the fast break drill. Then the gym door swings open and Coach Sheridan rushes through. His shirt is untucked and his hair is uncombed.

The fast break drill slows. Coach hurries over, tucking in his shirt with one hand and running the other hand through his hair.

"Okay, Knights. Let's go! Everybody over here," he says, circling his hands over his head. The team gathers around.

"Hey, Coach," Davonn says in a teasing voice. "You're late. Give me five wind sprints."

I almost jump out of my skin. I know Davonn is the star of the team and just fooling around, but no way I would ever do that. I mean, you don't want to mess with Coach Sheridan.

But Coach doesn't get mad at Davonn. He flashes a tired smile and says, "Okay, you're right. I'm late. But I've got two really good excuses. My wife had twins this morning. I'm a dad."

The team bursts into cheers and high fives.

"All right!"

"That's a BIG win!"

"Let's hear it for Coach Dad!"

"What did you have?" Bryce asks.

"Two boys."

More cheers. More high fives.

"What are their names?" Cammy asks.

"Liam and Aidan."

Davonn laughs. "Hey, three more and you'll have a starting five."

Coach shakes his head. I notice the dark circles around his eyes. He looks like he hasn't slept for days.

"I'm just happy to have a healthy back-court for right now." He holds up his hand. "Listen, guys. I'm exhausted. And I have to go back to the hospital in about an hour. Why don't we skip all the drills and just scrimmage?"

The team bursts into cheers again. The cheers for the scrimmage may be louder and longer than the cheers for the babies.

"Whites against Blues?" Davonn asks.

"I don't know. Why don't we mix it up this time?" Coach looks around the gym. "How about Link, Bryce, Anthony, Richie, and Grady on one team. Davonn, Mason, Quinton, C. J., and Ray on the other. I'll sub in Theo and Scott."

He points over to the scorer's table. "Madison, you and Cammy keep the score and the stats, please. I'll call the game. First team that scores twenty points wins."

The scrimmage game starts. Link wins the tip and gets the ball to Bryce, who passes it to Grady. He drives by Ray and dishes to me on the wing.

Shooter's got to shoot. The ball rattles around the rim, bumps against the backboard, and falls in. Lucky.

We take the lead, 2–0.

The next time down the floor, C. J. is all over me. I flip a pass to Link, who has his back to the basket. The big seventh grader fakes left and spins right. The ball goes off the backboard and through the net, pushing the score to 4–0.

But that doesn't last long. Davonn gets

untracked and sparks a comeback. Soon we're trailing 12–10.

Then Grady finds me open. My foot is just beyond the three-point line. I let it fly. *Swish!* We're up, 13–12.

"Game to twenty; losers have to run sprints!" Coach calls out from the sidelines. I notice he's not running the court the way he usually does. This deal about becoming a father must be pretty tough.

We trade baskets. A twisting, off-balance jumper by Davonn cuts our lead to one, 19–18.

Grady brings the ball down the court slowly. Everyone on our team is pumped up.

"One more basket!"

"Move it around!"

"Get a good shot!"

C. J.'s hand darts out and sends the ball skidding across the floor. I don't think. I just react, diving full-length across the floor, stretching for the ball. I can feel the floor scratching and tearing against my knees as they scrape against the court. My fingers grab hold of the ball and I push an awkward pass to Grady, who flips a pass to Bryce for a short jumper.

Swish! It's good. We win 21–18!

"All right, losers give me five and then take a break."

I stand on the sidelines slapping five with Bryce, Tony, Link, and Grady. "Way to go with the clutch bucket!" I say to Bryce. "Looks like *you're* the shooter now."

"I can't get the basket if you don't get the loose ball," he says.

I think about that one for a second. "I guess you're right. Maybe Coach should play us together more often. We make a pretty good team."

CHAPTER 17

Mallon!" Coach catches me by surprise. We're only a couple of minutes into our game against the Fair Hill Falcons and he's already calling my name. Maybe because we're down 6–2.

"Go in for C. J.," he says, pushing me toward the scorer's table. "Move the ball around and look for your shot."

I toss my warm-up shirt under the bench and report. "Mallon in for Jackson."

Cammy looks up from her scorebook. "Kind of early, aren't you?"

"I'm just doing what Coach tells me."

When I go in at the next whistle I'm jumping into that rushing river again. Fair Hill is good...*very* good. They move the ball with crisp confidence on offense and really put the clamps on you on defense. No wonder they beat us 53–36 last time we played.

I struggle to keep up. Everything is moving too fast. I miss two shots in a row and start worrying that Coach will yank me out of the game before I break a sweat. Now we're trailing by eight, 14–6.

Coach Sheridan jumps to his feet and shouts, "Timeout!"

We step off the court with our heads down. Coach is on us right away.

"Come on, we have to dig in! We're falling too far behind," he says. "We need to take care of the ball and tighten up on defense."

He looks around the circle of players. I know what he's thinking: *Who's going to play?* I start getting nervous that he's going to put C. J. back in. I make sure I look up. No way he's going to play someone with his head hanging down.

"Link and Ray," he says finally, "go in for Mason and Grady."

All right, I tell myself. *He's giving some*

more playing time to some Blue team players.

"We have the ball, so let's run an isolation play for Davonn on the right side." Coach points toward the court. "Davonn, if you get a chance, take it to the hoop. You might get fouled."

Davonn follows orders and takes the ball to the basket. The Fair Hill center bangs against Davonn as he lets the shot go. The ball bounces around, hangs on the rim, and falls in. The basket is good and Davonn goes to the line.

He hits the foul shot and we're only down 14–9.

Link grabs a rebound and tosses a quick outlet pass to Ray to work the fast break. The little seventh-grade point guard races up the middle of the court with Davonn and me on the sides. Fair Hill is watching Davonn, so Ray slips me the ball. I take it up strong just like in layup drills.

It's good. We've closed the gap to 14–11.

I'm in the rhythm of the game. I grab a long rebound, turn, and dribble upcourt with Ray and Davonn. I'm thinking about pulling up for a jumper at the foul line, but I slip a pass to Davonn, who cuts to the basket for an easy bucket.

It's 14–13. We're right back in the game.

I play most of the first half. I hit a three-pointer (my shot is coming around) and get my share of rebounds and assists. Still, we're behind 28–25 at the half. Like I said, the Fair Hill Falcons are good.

Coach surprises everyone, including me, when we start the second half. "Why don't we start off with Link, Davonn, Bryce, Grady, and Richie."

Bryce shoots me a quick glance and a nod. Davonn does the same. I'm starting. Finally.

"Mason and C. J.," Coach adds. "Be ready to come in."

Yeah, I'm starting. But I'd better play well if I want to stay in.

"We need a good start in the second half," Coach says, clapping his hands. "We don't want to fall too far behind these guys."

We get off to a good start. Davonn scores, and the next time we have the ball I slip a pass to Link underneath. His hook shot rolls around the rim and goes in.

"That's my boy!" Link's mother screams from the front row. "That's my boy!"

Fair Hill bounces back and grabs the lead with two quick baskets. After that we trade a few more. Coach puts in Mason and C. J. for Link and me. They keep it fairly close. But then we start slipping behind again. Fair Hill is up 45–40 when Coach calls my number again.

"Richie, go in for Davonn," he says.

"Davonn?" I say, but I'm thinking, *I'm not a forward.*

"He's going to need a couple of minutes to catch his breath."

I report to the scorer's table. "Did you say Davonn?" Cammy asks. Her face says it all.

"Are you sure?" Madison chimes in.

"Yeah, Coach wants me to go in for Davonn."

I have to guard a taller Fair Hill forward. They get the ball to him right away, but I hang tough and force him to take a bad shot. Then I make sure I get my body between him and the basket as I grab the rebound.

Maybe I can *be a forward,* I think as I pass off. *For a couple of minutes.*

Back on offense, I keep moving. The big Fair Hill forward doesn't want to chase me enough to cover me on the outside. Ray gets me a pass deep in the corner, behind the three-point line. I let it fly. *Swish!* We're back in the game, 45–43.

We get another stop on defense. I work my way open for another three-pointer. The ball bounces high off the back rim and falls in. Lucky shot, but I'll take it.

We're ahead 46–45 and the Fair Hill coach is calling a timeout.

I can hear him yelling, "Who's got the shooter?" as we hustle over to the sidelines. I can't help smiling when I hear that. It feels like old times.

Our bench is alive.

"All right, comeback time!"

"Way to shoot, Richie!"

"Go, Knights!"

Coach Sheridan settles us down. "Lots of time left. Davonn, report in for C. J. And Richie, switch back to guard. Good shooting.

Let's keep doing what we're doing. Good defense. Rebound. Move the ball on offense. Let's go."

I look up at the scoreboard as I walk back onto the court.

VISITOR   FAIR HILL
46   3:15   QTR 4   45

The lead bounces back and forth like a Ping-Pong ball. Neither team is able to get more than a basket ahead. With a minute to go, Davonn hits a tough in-your-face jumper with two Fair Hill defenders all over him.

We're ahead 54–53 with forty-five seconds to go. Our bench is up, chanting, "De-fense! De-fense! De-fense!"

My heart is pounding and my breath is speeding up. "Come on, let's play D!" I shout. But it's more to calm myself down than anything else.

Fair Hill works the ball around, watching the clock and looking for an opening. With just twelve seconds left, their big forward spins into the lane and puts up a shot.

Tweeeeeeeeeet! The referee blows his whistle as the ball bounces off the rim.

"Foul on number 35."

That's five fouls on Mason. He's out of the game and Link is back in.

Our coach calls for a timeout. He wants to freeze the shooter, make him nervous. It doesn't work. When play resumes, the big Fair Hill forward walks to the line and calmly drops two shots through the net. Clutch.

We're behind 55–54 with only ten seconds to go.

Bryce passes the ball in to Grady, who dribbles furiously upcourt. The rest of the team tries to find an open spot. The crowd and our bench are counting the clock down.

"Seven...six...five..."

I cut through the middle and lose my defender in the confusion. *I hope Grady sees me.* He does.

"Four...three...two..."

I have the ball. I'm open on the wing. I feel the game slow down as I go up for the jump shot. I can feel the ball. I can see the rim. Just like in the first Saratoga game. I can sense the crowd on their feet.

I spy Link open underneath...and snap a pass to him.

"One!"

Link shoots and the ball slips through the net as the buzzer sounds.

The bench and the crowd rush out onto the floor. It's like a wave crashing around me. But above it all I can hear Link's mom:

"That's my boy!"

CHAPTER 18

I'm standing outside the path that leads to Stone Creek Park. The trees are just beginning to bud. The Saturday morning air is cool but I can feel spring trying to push winter away.

I pace back and forth on the sidewalk near the opening to the park. I pull my phone out of my sweatpants to check the time. It's 10:04.

"Hey, sorry I'm late!" Cammy shouts, waving her hand over her head. She jogs up to me. "My dad was asking me a million questions."

"No worries. Are you ready to run?"

"That's what I'm here for. Lacrosse starts in a couple of weeks."

We walk down a narrow path toward the creek, pushing the overhanging limbs out of our way. We stop on the edge of a wider dirt path.

"Which way do we go?" Cammy asks.

I look both ways. "The left's a little harder, more uphill in spots. The right's a little easier."

Cammy smiles. "We'd better go to the right."

We start out. The ground is level. It is one of the easiest stretches of the path. I'm running at an even stride, a little slower than when I run with Bryce. Cammy picks up the pace. I step on it to catch up.

"How long is the trail?" she asks.

"About three miles. We can stop and walk if you get tired."

"I won't get tired."

We run side by side, zipping by some walkers and a few dogs. I point out some water by the side of the trail. "That was frozen over the last time Bryce and I ran."

"Where is Bryce?"

"He went to the batting cage with a bunch of kids. He's going to play baseball this spring."

"Are you going to try out?"

"Nah. Baseball's not my sport. I'm not very good. I can't hit a curve to save my life."

"You weren't much of a passer or a rebounder either, and look what happened." We run a little farther. "And your shot came back," Cammy adds.

I don't say anything. But I'm smiling inside, remembering the Plaza Middle School Knights' 9–1 season. It wasn't 10–0 like I predicted to Bryce, but we tied for first place in the conference. Not too bad. Coach Sheridan even started me in the last two games of the season.

"Watch out for that rock!" I shout.

Cammy sidesteps the rock jutting out of the dirt without breaking stride. She can run. We cross a stone bridge with the water gurgling under us. A man throws a stick into the water. His dog bounds in after it.

"Why don't you play lacrosse?" Cammy asks.

"I don't know how. I've never played."

"That doesn't matter. A lot of kids are just getting started. Anyway, a guy who shoots like you should be fine once you learn how to handle the stick. You'd probably score a million goals."

"Wait a second," I protest. "I'm not just a shooter. I got a whole bunch of rebounds and assists. At least in the second half of the season."

"You don't have to tell me," Cammy says. "I kept the stats, remember?"

"I even played defense against that big guy from Fair Hill when Davonn was out."

"Okay, okay." Cammy laughs as we cross the street that cuts through the park and run deeper into the woods. "You're *not* the shooter."

I never thought I would say this but...I like the sound of that.

THE REAL STORY: GREAT SHOOTERS

Richie is right. Ever since Dr. James Naismith invented the game of basketball in December 1891 in Springfield, Massachusetts, the team that scores the most points always wins. So teams have always needed players who can put the ball in the basket: the shooters, the players who know when the ball leaves their hand it's going in the bucket.

In the early days of basketball, players didn't use the jump shots we see in today's game. Instead they used the two-handed set shot. A player pushed the ball up from his or her chest with two hands. It might seem funny to us now, but some players were dead-eyes with that shot.

The jump shot came along in the 1930s and 40s. Kenny Sailors invented the new shot for a reason any kid can understand. Sailors played basketball with his older brother when he was growing up on a farm in Wyoming. Bud Sailors was six feet five inches tall, and Kenny got tired of his taller brother blocking most of his shots.

"I got to thinking that if I could dribble up to him—I was a pretty good dribbler—and then just jump as high as I could in the air and shoot the ball that I may not make it but at least I would try," Sailors recalled many years later. "When it went in the first couple of times, my brother said, 'Kenny, that's a good shot...you have to develop that.' I was clear up above him when I shot the ball."

Sailors took his jump shot to the University of Wyoming, where he was a three-time All-American, and helped the Cowboys win the 1943 national collegiate title, beating Georgetown 46–34.

A picture of Sailors and his jump shot appeared on the January 1946 cover of *LIFE*, the most popular magazine in the United

States at the time. Soon players all over the country were abandoning the old-fashioned two-handed set shot for Sailors's jump shot.

When the National Basketball Association (NBA) came along in 1946, the professional teams were already on the lookout for great shooters. The Boston Celtics won eleven NBA championships in thirteen seasons (1956 to 1969) with such Hall of Fame stars as center Bill Russell, playmaking guard Bob Cousy, and all-around hustler John Havlicek.

But the Celtics always had a great shooter. Bill Sharman was a sharpshooting guard from 1950 to 1961. Sharman led the NBA in foul shot percentage seven of his eleven seasons in the league.

After Sharman retired, the Celtics' best outside shooter was Sam Jones. The six-foot-four guard from North Carolina Central University was an important part of ten championship teams, hitting more than 45 percent of his shots from the field and more than 80 percent of his free throws.

Great shooters became even more important with the introduction of the three-point shot. For more than thirty years in the NBA, a shot from the court—anywhere on the court—only counted for two points. It didn't matter whether the player took the shot right under the basket or way past midcourt. Every shot counted the same.

The first professional basketball league to use a three-point shot—a shot past a certain distance counted for three points instead of two points—was the old American Basketball League (ABL). However, the ABL and the three-point shot did not last long.

A few years later another new professional league, the American Basketball Association (ABA), adopted the three-point shot. The ABA tried lots of things to make their games more exciting than the NBA, including red, white, and blue basketballs and slam-dunk contests.

When four teams from the ABA merged with the NBA in 1976, the three-point shot was left behind...for a few years. The NBA finally adopted the long shot before the 1979–1980 season. "Downtown" Freddie Brown of the Seattle SuperSonics led the league by making more than 44 percent of his shots from behind the three-point arc that season.

Gradually the three-point shot became a bigger part of the game. Hall of Fame players—Larry Bird, Reggie Miller, and John Stockton, for example—began to take and make more long shots. Other players such as Steve Kerr, Ray Allen, and Kyle Korver began to specialize in stretching the defense and shooting the three-pointer.

Maybe the greatest shooter ever is Stephen Curry of the Golden State Warriors. During the 2015–2016 NBA season, Curry shattered the record for most three-pointers in a season. The slender, six-foot-three guard from Davidson College sank an amazing 402 shots from beyond the arc. (Curry had held the previous regular season record with 286 three-pointers.)

Curry, who can shoot from anywhere on the court, has hit more than 44 percent of his three-pointers so far in his career. Curry can also get it done from the foul line. He's sunk more than 90 percent of his free throws.

But as Cammy told Richie, even the great shooters listed above could do more than shoot the ball. They were not "just" shooters.

For example, Celtics superstar Larry Bird grabbed an average of ten rebounds a game during his thirteen-year career. Bird was also a terrific passer for a big (six feet, nine inches) man, dishing out more than six assists a game.

John Stockton is the all-time NBA assists leader. He led the league in assists for nine consecutive seasons. Stockton may have hit more than 51 percent of his shots during his nineteen-year career with the Utah Jazz, but he also knew when to pass the ball to a teammate.

And as Cammy pointed out, Steph Curry is also a very good passer and an amazing dribbler. Curry distributes almost seven assists a game. He can play some defense too. The world's best shooter led the NBA in steals during the 2014–2015 and 2015–2016 seasons.

Stephen Curry isn't just a shooter, he plays the whole game.

ACKNOWLEDGMENTS

The author would like to thank Dan Harwood, the varsity basketball coach at Magruder High School in Rockville, Maryland. Coach Harwood was kind enough to allow me to observe his team practice for several days. Many of the descriptions of the practices and drills in the book came from watching the Magruder team. I was watching one of the best in action. Coach Harwood's teams have won two Maryland state 4A championships.

The information concerning Kenny Sailors and his invention of the jump shot contained in the Real Story is from the January 30, 2016, obituaries in the *New York Times* and *Washington Post* and a posting on *NCAA.com*.

The statistics contained in the Real Story come from the essential basketball website: *basketball-reference.com*.

ABOUT THE AUTHOR

Fred Bowen was a Little Leaguer who loved to read. Now he is the author of many action-packed books of sports fiction. He has also written a weekly sports column for kids in the *Washington Post* since 2000.

Fred played lots of sports growing up, including soccer at Marblehead High School. For thirteen years, he coached kids' baseball, soccer, and basketball teams. Some of his stories spring directly from his coaching experience and his sports-happy childhood in Marblehead, Massachusetts.

Fred holds a degree in history from the University of Pennsylvania and a law degree from George Washington University. He was a lawyer for many years before retiring to become a full-time children's author. Bowen has been a guest author at schools and conferences across the country, as well as the Smithsonian Institute in Washington, D. C., and The Baseball Hall of Fame.

Fred lives in Silver Spring, Maryland, with his wife Peggy Jackson. Their son is a college baseball coach, and their daughter is a reading teacher in Washington, D. C.

For more information
check out the author's website at
www.fredbowen.com.

HEY, SPORTS FANS!

Don't miss these action-packed books in the Fred Bowen Sports Story series!

 BASEBALL

Dugout Rivals
PB: $6.95 / 978-1-56145-515-7
Last year Jake was one of his team's best players. But this season it looks like a new kid is going to take Jake's place as team leader. Can Jake settle for second-best?

The Golden Glove
PB: $6.95 / 978-1-56145-505-8
Without his lucky glove, Jamie doesn't believe in his ability to lead his baseball team to victory. How will he learn that faith in oneself is the most important equipment for any game?

The Kid Coach
PB: $6.95 / 978-1-56145-506-5
Scott and his teammates can't find an adult to coach their team, so they must find a leader among themselves.

Perfect Game
PB: $6.95 / 978-1-56145-625-3
HC: $14.95 / 978-1-56145-701-4
Isaac is determined to pitch a perfect game—no hits, no runs, no walks, and no errors. He gets close a couple of times, but when things go wrong he can't get his head back in the game. Then Isaac meets an interesting Unified Sports basketball player who shows him a whole new way to think about perfect.

Playoff Dreams
PB: $6.95 / 978-1-56145-507-2
Brendan is one of the best players in the league, but no matter how hard he tries, he can't make his team win.

T. J.'s Secret Pitch
PB: $6.95 / 978-1-56145-504-1
T. J.'s pitches just don't pack the power they need to strike out the batters, but the story of 1940s baseball hero Rip Sewell and his legendary eephus pitch may help him find a solution.

Throwing Heat
PB: $6.95 / 978-1-56145-540-9
HC: $14.95 / 978-1-56145-573-7
Jack throws the fastest pitches around, but lately his blazing fastballs haven't been enough. He's got to learn new pitches to stay ahead of the batters. But can he resist bringing the heat?

Winners Take All
PB: $6.95 / 978-1-56145-512-6
Kyle makes a poor decision to cheat in a big game. Someone discovers the truth and threatens to reveal it. What can Kyle do now?

 BASKETBALL

The Final Cut
PB: $6.95 / 978-1-56145-510-2
Four friends realize that they may not all make the team and that the tryouts are a test—not only of their athletic skills, but also of their friendship.

Full Court Fever
PB: $6.95 / 978-1-56145-508-9
The Falcons have the skill but not the height to win their games. Will the full-court zone press be the solution to their problem?

Hardcourt Comeback
PB: $6.95 / 978-1-56145-516-4
Brett blew a key play in an important game. Now he feels like a loser for letting his teammates down—and he keeps making mistakes. How can Brett become a "winner" again?

Off the Rim
PB: $6.95 / 978-1-56145-509-6
Hoping to be more than a benchwarmer, Chris learns that defense is just as important as offense.

On the Line
PB: $6.95 / 978-1-56145-511-9
Marcus is the highest scorer and the best rebounder, but he's not so great at free throws—until the school custodian helps him overcome his fear of failure.

Outside Shot
PB: $6.95 / 978-1-56145-956-8
HC: $14.95 / 978-1-56145-955-1
Eighth-grader Richie Mallon has always known he was a shooter. He has practiced every day at his driveway hoop, perfecting his technique. Now that he is facing basketball tryouts under a tough new coach, will his amazing shooting talent be enough to keep him on the team?

Real Hoops
PB: $6.95 / 978-1-56145-566-9
Hud can run, pass, and shoot at top speed. But he's not much of a team player. Can Ben convince Hud to leave his dazzling—but one-man—style back on the asphalt?

⬤ FOOTBALL

Double Reverse
PB: $6.95 / 978-1-56145-807-3
HC: $14.95 / 978-1-56145-814-1
The season starts off badly, and things get even worse when the Panthers quarterback is injured. Jesse knows the playbook by heart, but he feels that he's too small for the role. He just doesn't look the part. Can he play against type and help the Panthers become a winning team?

Quarterback Season
PB: $6.95 / 978-1-56145-594-2
Matt expects to be the starting quarterback. But after a few practices watching Devro, a talented seventh grader, he's starting to get nervous. To make matters worse, his English teacher is on his case about a new class assignment: a journal.

Touchdown Trouble
PB: $6.95 / 978-1-56145-497-6
Thanks to a major play by Sam, the Cowboys beat their archrivals to remain undefeated. But the celebration ends when Sam and his teammates make an unexpected discovery. Is their perfect season in jeopardy?

SOCCER

Go for the Goal!
PB: $6.95 / 978-1-56145-632-1
Josh and his talented travel league soccer teammates are having trouble coming together as a successful team—until he convinces them to try team-building exercises.

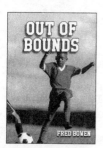

Out of Bounds
PB: $6.95 / 978-1-56145-894-3
HC: $14.95 / 978-1-56145-845-5
During a game against the Monarchs, Nate has to decide between going for a goal after a player on the rival team gets injured, or kicking the ball out of bounds as an act of good sportsmanship. What is the balance between playing fair and playing your best?

Soccer Team Upset
PB: $6.95 / 978-1-56145-495-2
Tyler is angry when his team's star player leaves to join an elite travel team. Just as Tyler expected, the Cougars' season goes straight downhill. Can he make a difference before it's too late?